How to use this book

1 Cut each page from the book.

Then cut along the T-shaped line to separate each section of the page so it is easier for your child to handle the pieces.

This book is structured so your child will advance gradually from easy to challenging activities. The activities are arranged according to difficulty based on the number of parts, the different sizes and shapes of the parts, and the amount of folding. We encourage your child to complete the activities in the order presented. However, it is okay to create whichever craft your child likes as long as he or she is capable of completing it.

2 Cut the parts, then paste them on the base.

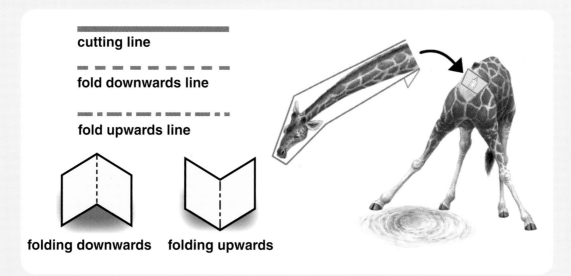

cutting line

fold downwards line

fold upwards line

folding downwards   folding upwards

If your child has difficulty cutting or pasting, it is okay for you to help.

3 Play with the completed crafts.

When your child has completed a craft, please offer him or her lots of praise. Furthermore, please encourage your child to play with the craft and have fun.

Try to limit the number of pages your child will complete in a day. It is best to end the day's activity when your child still wants to do more.

You may also want to bind the completed crafts together like a book, or connect them like a poster. Your child may want to continue playing with his or her completed crafts and share them with others.

How to choose and hold scissors

Scissors can be dangerous if not handled properly. Keep an eye on your child when he or she is doing the cutting exercises.

How to choose a good pair of scissors

1 Choose safety scissors with round tips.

2 Choose scissors with holes that suit your child's hands and fingers.

3 Choose scissors your child can open and close easily.

▲ Please choose easy-to-use safety scissors. Pictured on the right are plastic safety scissors.

How to cut with scissors

Show your child how to put his or her thumb into the smaller hole and his or her forefinger and middle finger into the bigger hole of the scissors. If the bigger hole is large enough, have your child put his or her ring finger into the hole as well.

When your child holds scissors, please align his or her hand with the scissors so that they form a straight line when viewed from above.

▲ Please try to align your child's hand with the scissors so that they form a straight line.

How to choose glue and how to paste

If your child will be using glue for the first time, carefully select a type of glue that he or she will enjoy using.

Please choose a child-safe product in an easy-to-use container. Your child can use a glue stick but it is best for children to use glue that can be applied by hand. Children enjoy the tactile experience of spreading glue with their fingers.

▲ Please choose child-safe glue.

Tips for pasting

Line your table with scrap paper before your child starts. Have your child apply an appropriate amount of glue onto the tip of his or her middle finger and then spread it thinly on the part to be pasted. Please put the glue on the side with the glue symbol.

When your child is applying glue, encourage him or her to hold the part with one hand and apply the glue onto it with the other. This is difficult for young children, you can hold the paper for your child at first.

▲ Begin by placing glue onto the part. Then ask your child to use his or her finger to spread the glue on the designated area.

Tiger

■ Cut and fold the tiger, then paste it on the base to complete.
Play with the tiger to make it pounce.

● HOW TO CREATE AND PLAY

1. Cut along ▬▬▬.
Then fold upwards along —··—.

2. Paste the part on the base.

3. Move the part to make the tiger jump.

Tiger

A tiger usually hunts alone.

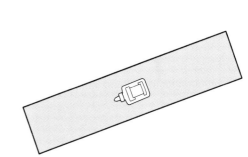

Glue the back.

Hedgehog

- Cut and fold the quills, then paste it on the base to complete.
  Play with the hedgehog to make it ruffle up its quills.

2

HOW TO CREATE AND PLAY

1. Cut along ▬▬ .
   Then fold upwards along ━ ‐ ━ ‐ .

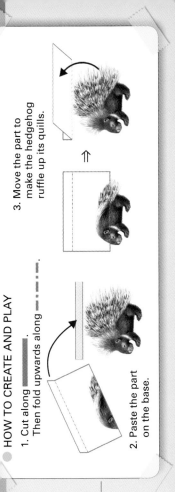

2. Paste the part on the base.

3. Move the part to make the hedgehog ruffle up its quills.

⇧

Hedgehog

A hedgehog ruffles its quills to defend itself.

Glue the back.

3 Hippopotamus

■ Cut and fold the face of the hippo, then paste it on the base to complete.
Play with the hippo to make it open its mouth wide.

● HOW TO CREATE AND PLAY

1. Cut along ▬▬▬.
   Then fold downwards along – – – –.

2. Paste the part on the base.

3. Move the part to make the hippo open its mouth wide.

Hippopotamus

A hippopotamus can open its mouth very wide.

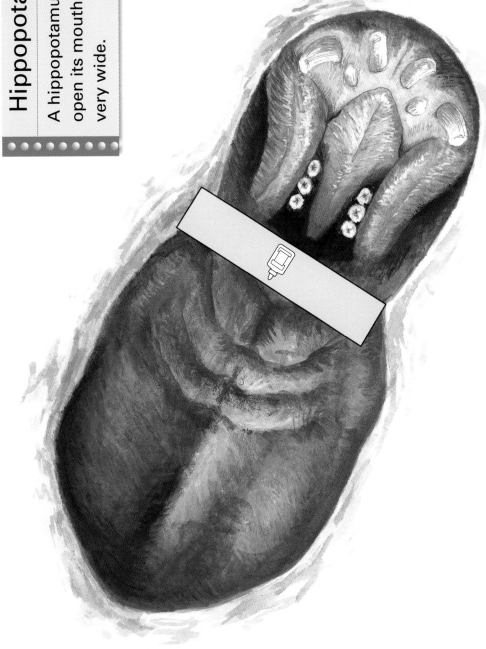

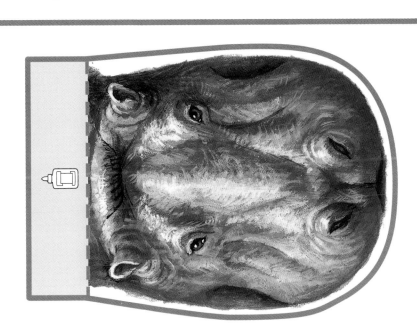

Giraffe

4

■ Cut and fold the neck of the giraffe, then paste it on the base to complete. Play with the giraffe to make it drink water.

1. Cut along _____.
   Then fold downwards along – – – –.

2. Paste the part on the base.

3. Move the part to make the giraffe drink water.

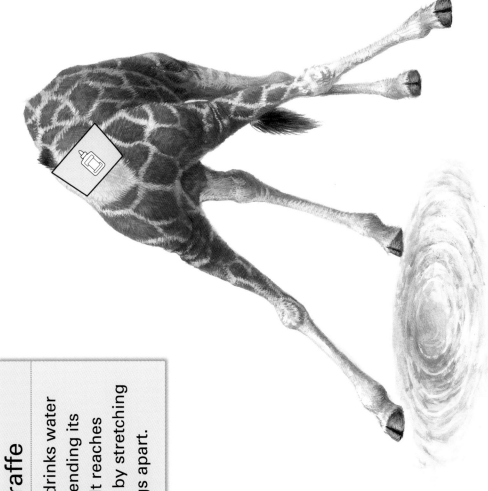

Giraffe

A giraffe drinks water without bending its forelegs. It reaches the water by stretching its forelegs apart.

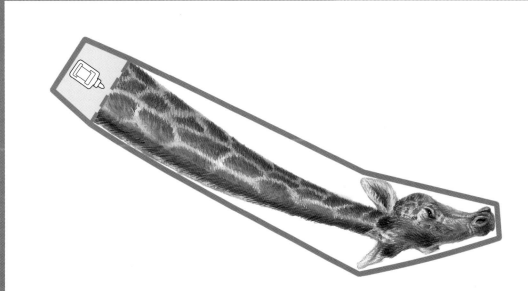

5

Sea Otter

■ Cut and fold the arms of the sea otter, then paste it on the base to complete.
Play with the sea otter to make it bang the clam against the stone.

HOW TO CREATE AND PLAY

1. Cut along ▬▬▬.
Then fold downwards along – – – –.

2. Paste the part on the base.

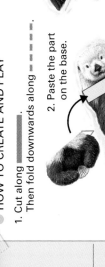

3. Move the part to make the sea otter bang the clam against the stone.

Sea Otter

A sea otter bangs clams against a stone on its chest to break the shells and then eat the meat.

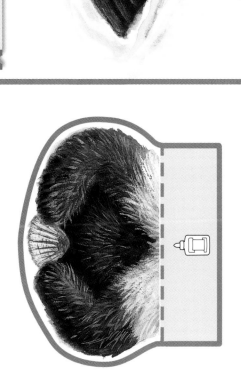

Flamingo

■ Cut and fold the neck and legs of the flamingo, then paste them on the base to complete. Play with the flamingo to make it sleep and stand on one leg only.

HOW TO CREATE AND PLAY

1. Cut along ____.
   Then fold upwards along — ·· — ··.

2. Paste the parts on the base.

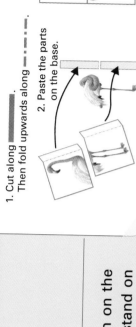

3. Move the parts to make the flamingo sleep and stand on one leg only.

⇑

Paste ① here

Paste ② here

Flamingo

A flamingo sleeps with one leg bent and its neck folded so it can lay its head on its back.

Glue the back on ① .

Glue the back on ② .

Alligator

Cut and fold the face and tail of the alligator, then paste them on the base to complete. Play with the alligator to make it open its mouth and swing its tail.

HOW TO CREATE AND PLAY

1. Cut along ——.
   Then fold downwards along – – –.

2. Paste the parts on the base.

3. Move the parts to make the alligator open its mouth and swing its tail.

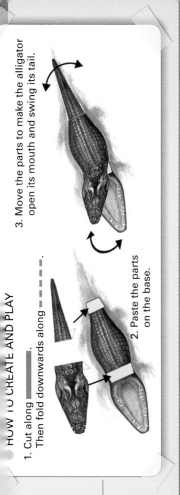

Alligator

An alligator has a powerful jaw. It can also open its mouth very wide.

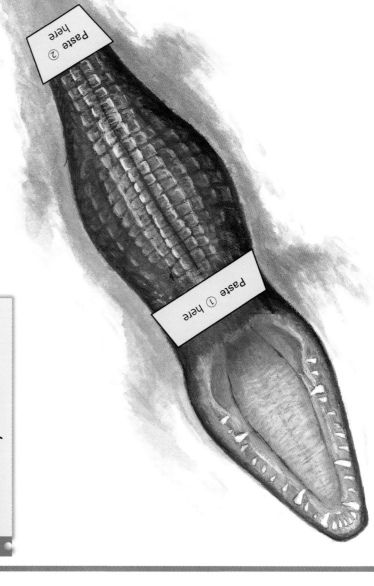

Paste ② here

Paste ① here

①

②

Gorilla

8

■ Cut and fold the arms of the gorilla, then paste them on the base to complete. Play with the gorilla to make it beat its chest with its hands.

1. Cut along ▬▬. Then fold downwards along – – –.

2. Paste the parts on the base.

...to make the gorilla beat its chest with its hands.

Gorilla

A gorilla will beat its chest with its hands to threaten enemies.

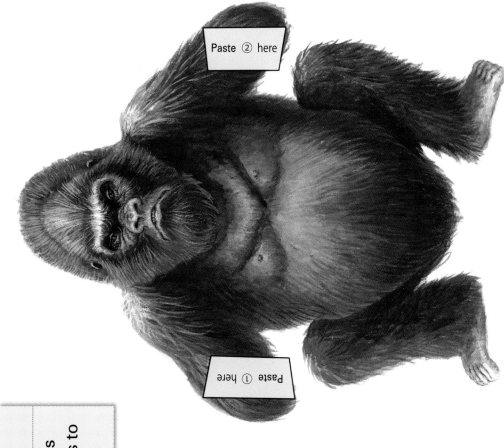

Paste ② here

Paste ① here

①

②

Raccoon

■ Cut and fold the arms of the raccoon, then paste them on the base to complete. Play with the raccoon to make it dunk the food in water.

1. Cut along ▬▬▬.
   Then fold downwards along ▬ ▬ ▬ ▬.

2. Paste the parts on the base.

Raccoon

A raccoon puts its food in water as if it is washing the food.

Paste ② here

Paste ① here

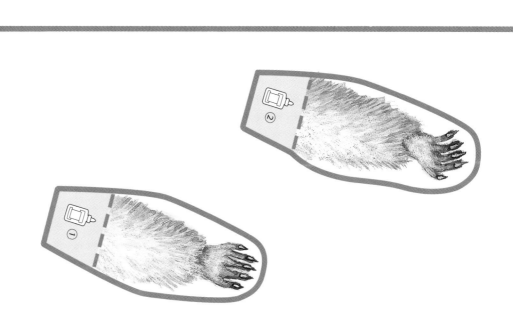

10 Panda

- Cut and fold the arms of the panda, then paste them on the base to complete. Play with the panda to make it eat bamboo leaves.

HOW TO CREATE AND PLAY

1. Cut along ———.
   Then fold downwards along – – – – –.

2. Paste the parts on the base.

3. Move the parts to make the panda eat bamboo leaves.

Paste ② here

Paste ① here

Panda

A panda can grip bamboo leaves with its paws.

①

②

11 Ostrich

■ Cut and fold the egg of the ostrich, then paste it on the base to complete.
Play with the ostrich egg to hatch the chick.

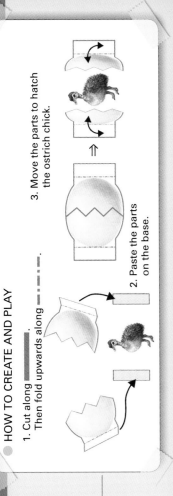

Ostrich

An ostrich's egg is very large. It is about twenty times larger than a chicken's egg.

Paste ② here

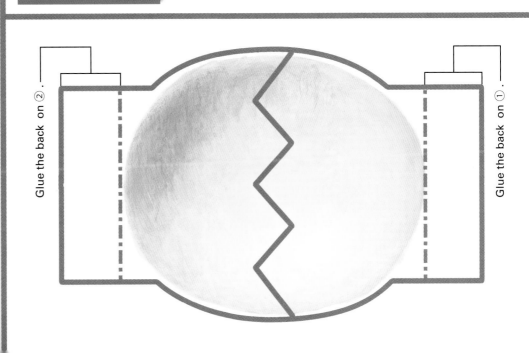

Paste ① here

Glue the back on ② .

Glue the back on ① .

12 Koala

■ Cut and fold the koalas, then paste them on the base to complete.
Play with the koalas to make them move up and down.

● HOW TO CREATE AND PLAY

1. Cut along _____.
   Then fold downwards along – – – –
   and upwards along – · – · – .

2. Paste the part on the base.

3. Move the part to make the koalas climb up and down.

Koala

A koala spends almost all day in a tree.

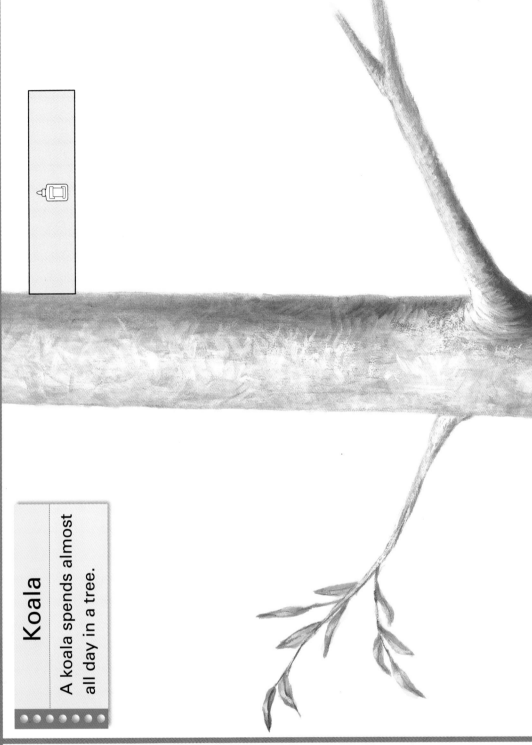

Glue the back.

13

Buffalo

■ Cut and fold the buffalo, then paste it on the base to complete.
Play with the buffalo to make it butt against the other buffalo.

● HOW TO CREATE AND PLAY

1. Cut along ▬▬▬ .
Then fold downwards along ▬ ▬ ▬
and upwards along ▬ · ▬ · ▬ .

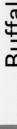

2. Paste the part
on the base.

3. Move the part to make
the buffalo butt against
the other buffalo.

Buffalo

Male buffalo fight
by butting their horns.

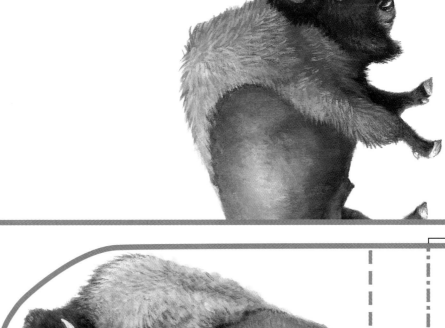

Glue the back.

14 Bear

- Cut and fold the arm of the bear, then paste it on the base to complete. Play with the bear to make it catch the fish.

● HOW TO CREATE AND PLAY

1. Cut along ▬▬▬.
   Then fold downwards along ▬ ▬ ▬
   and upwards along ▬ ∙ ▬ ∙ ▬ .

2. Paste the part on the base.

3. Move the part to make the bear catch the fish.

⇑

Bear

A bear catches fish with its forearms.

Glue the back.

15 Rhinoceros

■ Cut and fold the neck of the rhino, then paste it on the base to complete.
Play with the rhino to make it butt against the other rhino.

rhino butt the other rhino.

1. Cut along ▭.
   Then fold downwards along – – – –.
   and upwards along – ·· – ·· –.

2. Paste the part on the base.

Rhinoceros

A rhinoceros' horn is not a bone. It is made of the same material as fingernails.

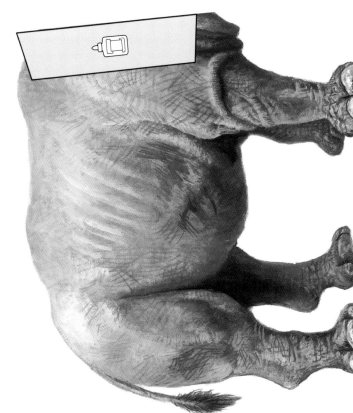

Glue the back.

16 Zebra

- Cut and fold the rear of the zebra, then paste it on the base to complete.
  Play with the zebra to make it kick its enemy.

HOW TO CREATE AND PLAY

1. Cut along ▬▬▬.
   Then fold downwards along ▬ ▬ ▬
   and upwards along ▬ · ▬ · ▬ .

2. Paste the part on the base.

3. Move the part to make the zebra kick its enemy.

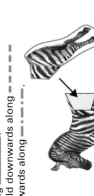

Zebra

A zebra defends itself by kicking with its hind legs.

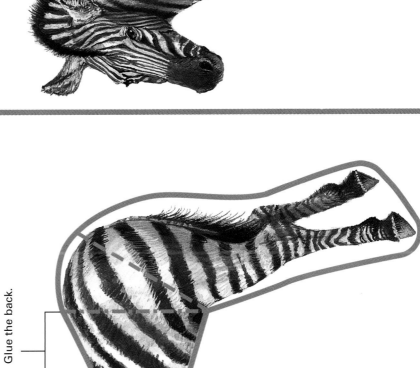

Glue the back.

Chameleon

■ Cut and fold the tongue of the chameleon, then paste it on the base to complete. Play with the chameleon to make it stretch its tongue and catch the insect.

● HOW TO CREATE AND PLAY

1. Cut along ▬▬▬.
   Then fold downwards along ▬ ▬ ▬
   and upwards along ▬ ∙ ▬ ∙ ▬.

2. Paste the part on the base.

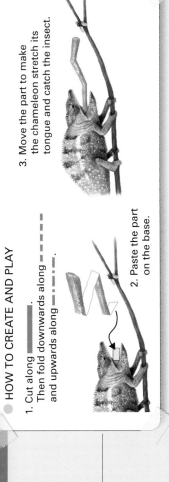

3. Move the part to make the chameleon stretch its tongue and catch the insect.

Chameleon

A chameleon stretches its sticky tongue to catch insects.

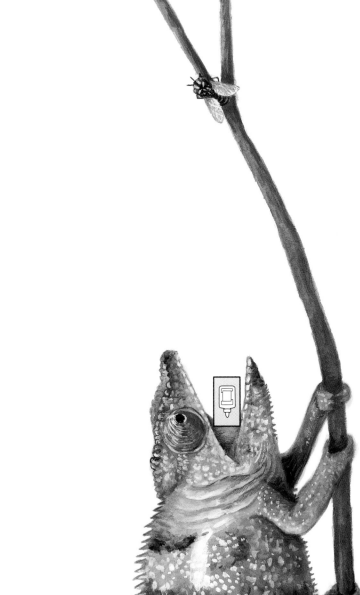

Fold downwards.

Fold upwards.

Fold downwards.

18 Camel

■ Cut and fold the camel, then paste it on the base to complete.
Play with the camel to make it sit down and stand up.

1. Cut along ▬▬▬.
Then fold downwards along ▬ ▬ ▬
and upwards along ▬ · ▬ · ▬.

2. Paste the part on the base.

3. Move the part to make the camel sit down and stand up.

⇑ ⇑

Camel

A camel has thick skin on its knees so it can sit on the hot desert sand.

Glue the back.

19 Elephant

■ Cut and fold the trunk and ears of the elephant, then paste them on the base to complete. Play with the elephant to make it wave its ears and trunk.

● HOW TO CREATE AND PLAY

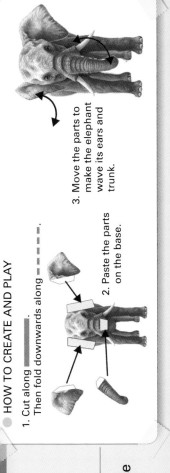

1. Cut along ▬▬▬.
   Then fold downwards along ╌ ╌ ╌.

2. Paste the parts on the base.

3. Move the parts to make the elephant wave its ears and trunk.

Elephant

An elephant waves its big ears to cool off.

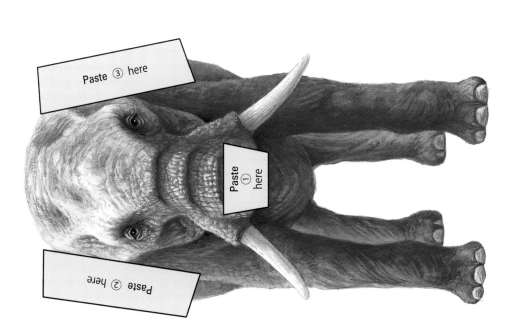

Paste ③ here

Paste ① here

Paste ② here

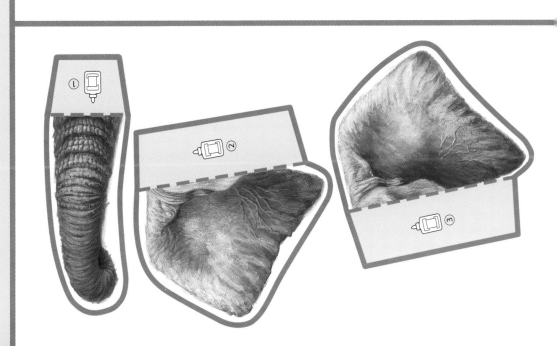

① ② ③

Chimpanzee

■ Cut, fold and paste the face of the chimpanzee, then paste the part on the base to complete. Play with the chimpanzee to make it smile.

1. Cut along ▬▬▬.
Then fold downwards along ▬ ▬ ▬
and upwards along ▬ · ▬ · ▬.

2. Glue the backs together.

3. Paste the part on the base.

4. Move the part to make the chimpanzee smile.

⇑

Chimpanzee

A chimpanzee can smile.

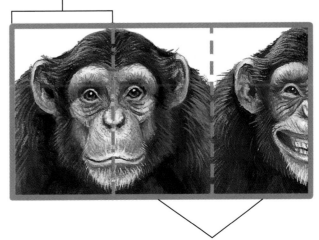

Glue the back on the base.

Glue the backs together.

21

Lion

■ Cut, fold and paste the face of the lion, then paste the part on the base to complete. Play with the lion to make it roar.

● HOW TO CREATE AND PLAY

1. Cut along ▬▬. Then fold downwards along ▬ ▬ ▬ and upwards along ▬·▬·▬.

2. Glue the backs together.

3. Paste the part on the base.

4. Move the part to make the lion roar.

⇑

Lion

A lion's roar is very loud. You can hear a lion's roar from several miles or kilometers away.

Glue the backs together.

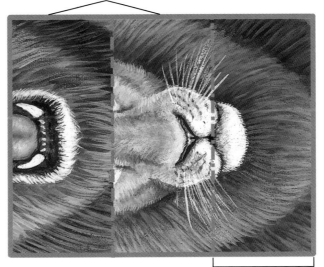

Glue the back on the base.

Owl

■ Cut, fold and paste the face of the owl, then paste the part on the base to complete. Play with the owl to make it turn its face.

1. Cut along _____.
   Then fold downwards along – – – –
   and upwards along ▬ ▪ ▬ ▪ ▬ .

2. Glue the backs together.

3. Paste the part on the base.

... move the part ... the owl turn its face.

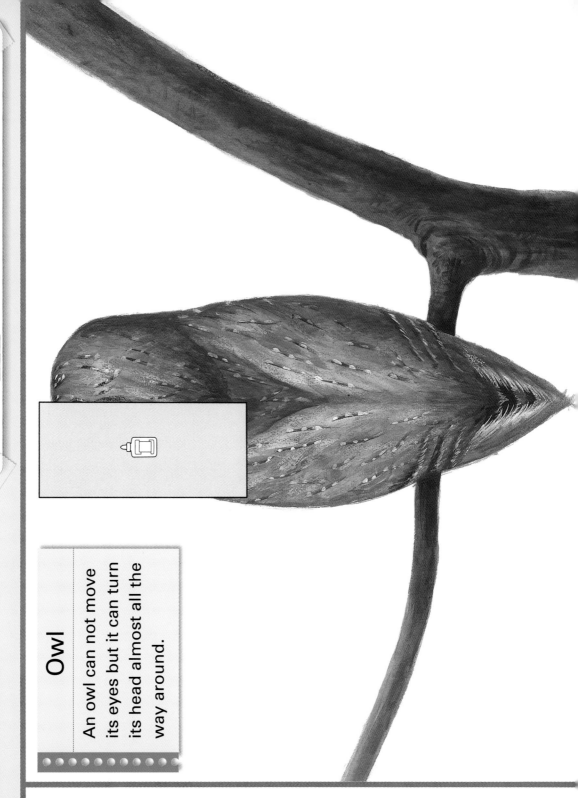

Owl

An owl can not move its eyes but it can turn its head almost all the way around.

Glue the back on the base.

Glue the backs together.

Squirrel

■ Cut, fold and paste the tail of the squirrel, then paste the part on the base to complete. Play with the squirrel to make it swish its tail.

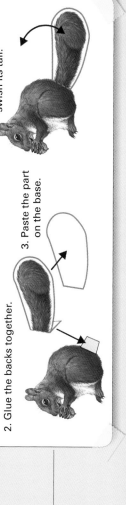

2. Glue the backs together.

3. Paste the part on the base.

swish its tail.

Squirrel

A squirrel keeps its balance and warms itself with its bushy tail.

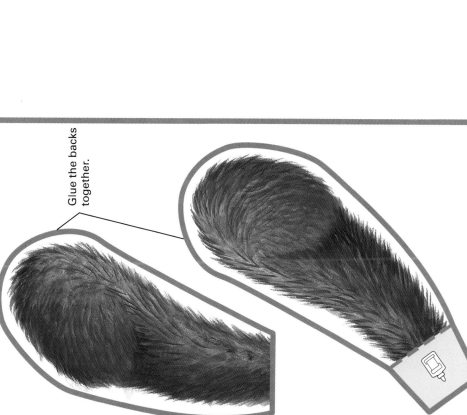

Glue the backs together.

24

Leopard

■ Cut, fold and paste the leopard, then paste the part on the base to complete. Play with the leopard to make it jump on the rock from the tree.

● HOW TO CREATE AND PLAY

1. Cut along ——— .
   Then fold downwards along — — — — and upwards along —··—··— .

2. Glue the backs together.

3. Paste the part on the base.

4. Move the part to make the leopard jump down from the tree.

⇑

Leopard

A leopard is good at climbing trees. It can pounce from above.

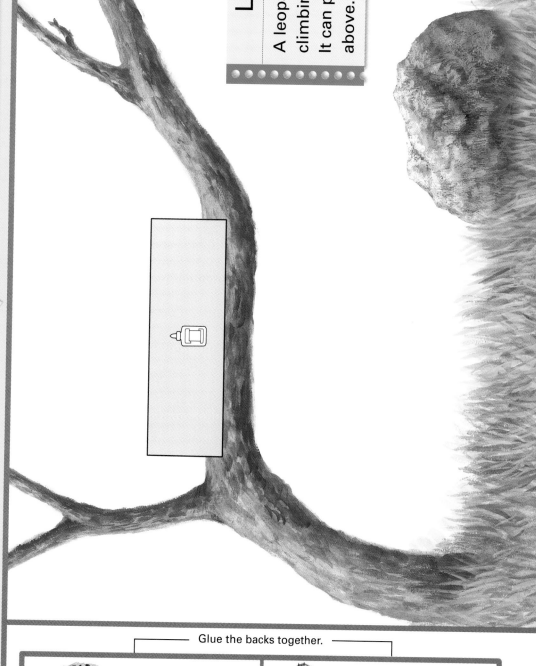

Glue the backs together.

Glue the back on the base.

Spider Monkey

■ Cut, fold and paste the spider monkey, then paste the part on the base to complete. Play with the spider monkey to make it swing from one tree to another.

1. Cut along ▬▬▬.
   Then fold upwards along ▬ · ▬ · ▬.

2. Glue the backs together.

3. Paste the part on the base.

The spider monkey swing from one tree to another.

Spider Monkey

A spider monkey can grip branches with its tail.

Glue the back on the base.

Glue the backs together.

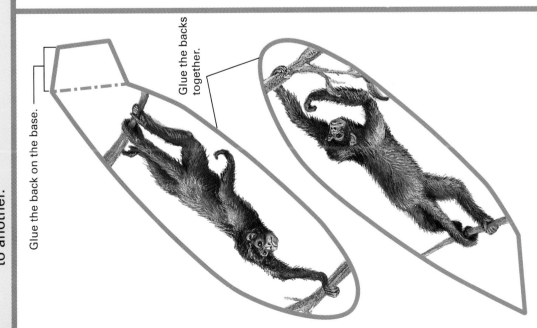

Sea Lion

■ Cut, fold and paste the ball, then paste the part on the base to complete.
Play with the ball to make the sea lions throw it back and forth.

97

HOW TO CREATE AND PLAY

1. Cut along ▬▬▬ .
   Then fold upwards along ▬ • ▬ .

2. Glue the backs together.

3. Paste the part on the base.

4. Move the part to make the sea lions play with the ball.

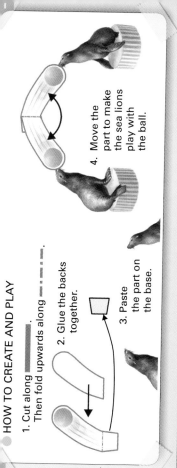

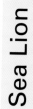

Sea Lion

Sea lions like to play.
Sea lions can learn many tricks.

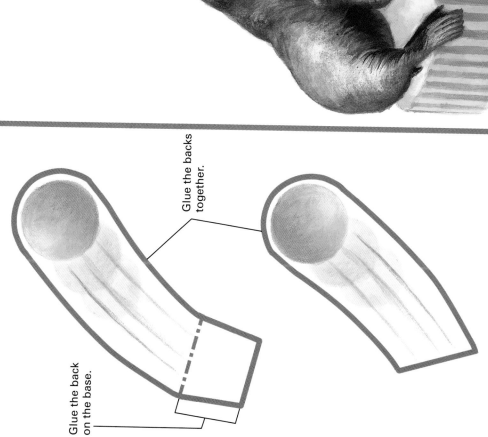

Glue the backs together.

Glue the back on the base.

Water Buffalo

■ Cut, fold and paste the tail of the water buffalo, then paste the part on the base to complete. Play with the water buffalo to make it swing its tail.

1. Cut along ——.
Then fold upwards along — · —.

2. Glue the backs together.

3. Paste the part on the base.

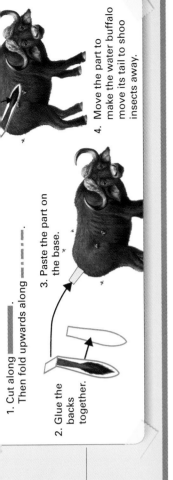

4. Move the part to make the water buffalo move its tail to shoo insects away.

Water Buffalo
A water buffalo waves its tail to shoo insects away.

Glue the back on the base.

Fold upwards.

Glue the backs together.

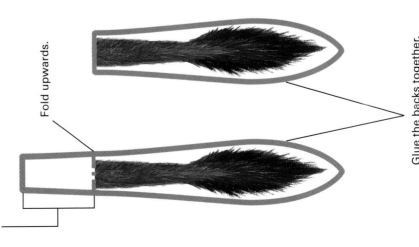

28 Cobra

■ Cut, fold and paste the parts on the base to complete. Play with the cobra to make it stretch its neck.

1. Cut along ▬▬▬.
Then fold downwards
along ▬ ▬ ▬
and upwards
along ▬·▬·▬.

2. Glue the backs together.

3. Paste the parts on the base.

4. Move the parts to make the cobra stretch its neck.

Cobra

A cobra will stretch its neck when threatened.

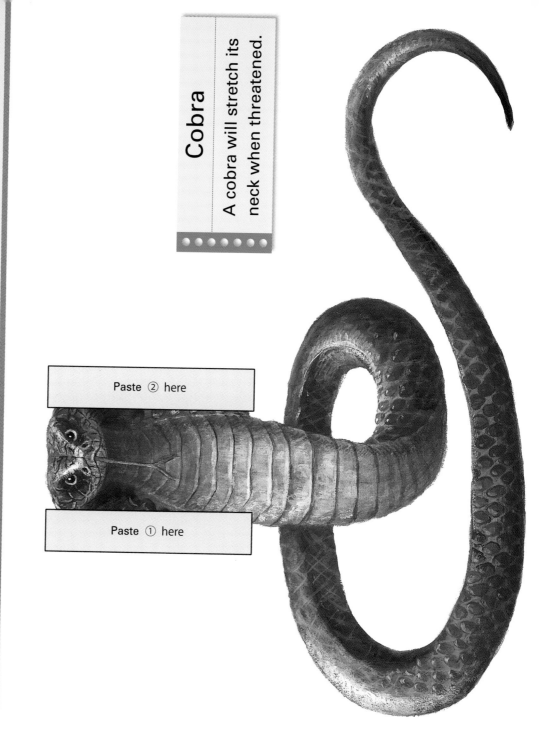

Paste ② here

Paste ① here

Glue the back on ①.

Glue the backs together.

Glue the backs together.

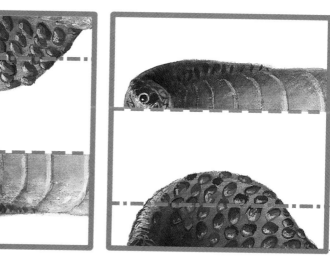

Glue the back on ②.

Kangaroo

■ Cut and fold the joey and the kangaroo pouch, then paste them on the base to complete. Play with the joey to make it go in and out of the pouch.

● HOW TO CREATE AND PLAY

1. Cut along ▬▬▬▬.
   Then fold downwards along ╌╌╌╌
   and upwards along ╌·╌·╌.

2. Paste the joey.
   Then paste the pouch.

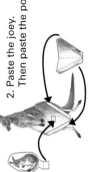

3. Move the part to make the joey go in and out of the pouch.

⇑

Kangaroo

A female kangaroo carries a joey in its pouch.

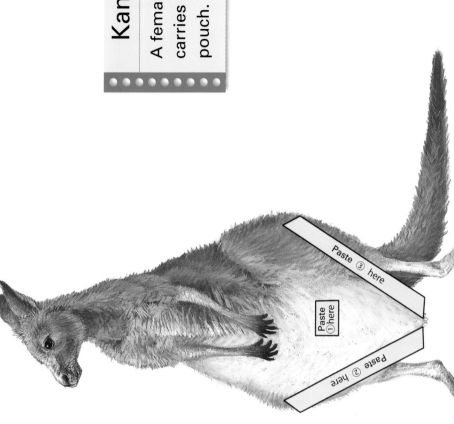

Paste ③ here

Paste ① here

Paste ② here

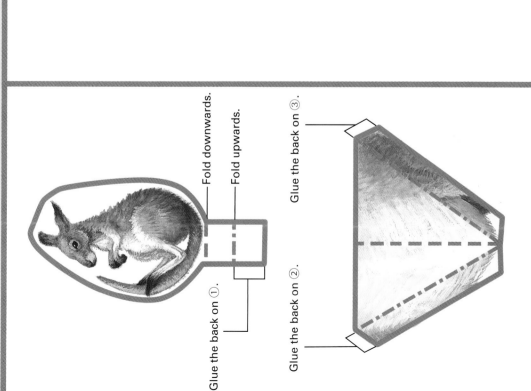

Fold downwards.

Fold upwards.

Glue the back on ①.

Glue the back on ②.

Glue the back on ③.

Peacock

■ Cut and fold the feathers of the peacock, then paste them on the base to complete. Play with the peacock to make it spread its feathers.

HOW TO CREATE AND PLAY

1. Cut along ▬▬▬ .
   Then fold downwards along ▬ ▬ ▬ and upwards along ▬ · ▬ · ▬ .

2. Paste the parts on the base.

3. Move the parts to make the peacock spread its feathers.

Peacock

A male peacock spreads his beautiful feathers for female peacocks to see.

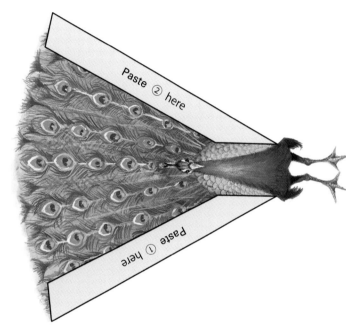

Paste ② here

Paste ① here

Glue the back on ① .

Glue the back on ② .

Certificate of Achievement

is hereby congratulated on completing

Paper Playtime: Animals

Presented on _____ ,20 _____

_____
Parent or Guardian